This book belongs to:

_____

For my dad, who gave me my love of machinery ~ J. L.

For Ernie of Wills Domain, whose tractors
and kindness inspired this book ~ D. B.

First published in Great Britain in 2021 by Andersen Press Ltd.,
20 Vauxhall Bridge Road, London SW1V 2SA
Originally published in Australia in 2019 as *All the Factors of Why I Love Tractors*
by Little Hare Books, an imprint of Hardie Grant Egmont.
Published by arrangement with Rights People, London.
Text copyright © Davina Bell 2019
Illustrations copyright © Jenny Løvlie 2019
The rights of Davina Bell and Jenny Løvlie to be identified as author and
illustrator of this work have been asserted by them in accordance with the
Copyright, Designs and Patents Act, 1988.
All rights reserved.
Printed and bound in China.
10 9 8 7 6 5 4 3 2 1
British Library Cataloguing in Publication Data available.
ISBN 978 1 83913 078 6

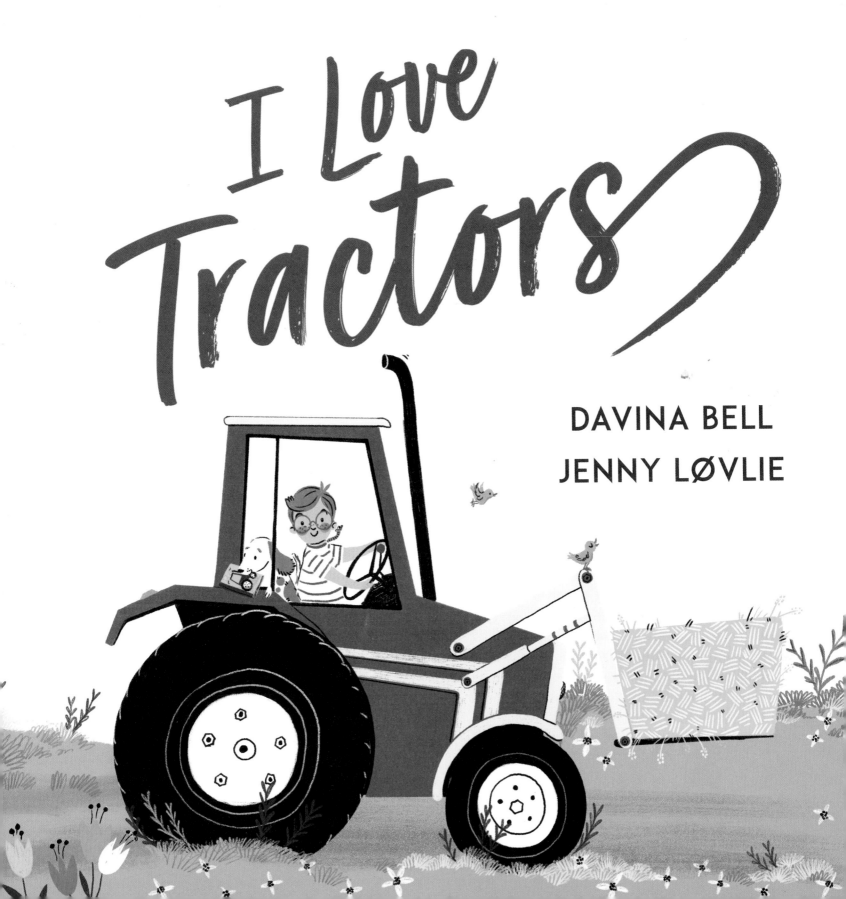

I Love Tractors

DAVINA BELL
JENNY LØVLIE

I'm off on an outing with Mama today,
and not just down to the park for a play.

Where are we going? Can you guess? Take a look!
(I will give you a hint and the hint is: a book.)

Down past the school and the pool and the shop, I run through the door with a skip and a hop.

The library!

"Hello there, Frankie McGee,"
Miss Squid, the librarian, whispers to me.

It's a place where you're not meant to shout, yell or cry,
so I whisper back, "Hi!" as I walk quickly by.

"**Oh no,**" says my mum with a very big groan
when I show her the book that I want to take home.

"There are more than a squillion good books here to try! Why is it always those tractors, Frank, **why?!**"

"Why, thank you for asking," I say with great glee.
"I'd love to explain why they're special to me,
and all of the various, glorious factors
that make up the love that I have for all tractors.

First...

Four big black tyres on wheels that can travel
through huge muddy fields or across pits of gravel.

A rumbling engine, a pipe that spits smoke,
a rake if you're raking, a hoe that can poke.

A seat for the farmer,
a wheel that she steers,
and a grumbling noise
as she changes the gears.

Levers and buttons
and pedals to press..."

"Trucks have those too," Mama loudly protests.

"A little more hush, thank you, Mrs McGee,"
the librarian calls. "Use your library voice, please."

I say softly, "But Mama, trucks just cannot do all the things that a tractor can, let me tell you.

A tractor has all different bits that attach:
a shovel for digging a vegetable patch;
a plough to turn earth so it's ready for seeds;
a sharp blade to chop all your troublesome weeds."

"Please stop," says my mum.
"I have heard quite enough."

"But I'm only beginning –
they do heaps
more stuff!"

"You used to like trains," my mother complains.

"But then I got bigger and so did my brains
and I realised trains only chug round on a track.
How boring – I'm snoring just thinking of that."

"Police cars have sirens! Gliders have wings!"

"And forklifts have forks if you're into those things.
But not one of those is a good enough factor
to challenge my love for a shiny red tractor,
like an old Massey Ferguson – what a machine!

Or if red's not around, well, I guess I'd take green.
It's the colour of tractors made by John Deere."

"I know," says my mum.
"I've been hearing all year.
What about...

... fire trucks with ladders and hoses?
Or planes with their wide wings and cute little noses.
Cranes are so tall – they can help build a wall!
They can lift things up high, they can lower and haul.
A cement mixer?"

"All it can do is go round."

"A steamroller?"

"Just sort of squashes the ground.
A mower for lawns is a big bunch of yawns,
and a trawler can only go trawling for prawns."

"What's wrong
with tractors?
I don't understand."

"Oh, Frank, I am sorry but I just can't stand
any more books about them. Will these do instead?
Cable cars, submarines, taxis – a sled?
This one has rockets high-flying in space.
Or that one has cars driving fast in a race."

"No thanks," I say in my most polite voice.
"But I think you will be very pleased with my choice.

I'll lend it to you if you're interested too.
There's so much you could learn about what tractors do."

"FRANKIE!" yells Mama.

"HUSH!" says Miss Squid.
"Did you find something, Frank?"

"Why, yes, yes I did.

For many and various, glorious factors...

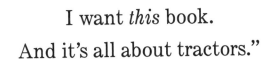

I want *this* book.
And it's all about tractors."

"What a surprise – I would never have guessed,"
says Miss Squid with a wink. "Well, you know yourself best.
When you want something different, just come and find me.
A boy who likes books is a nice thing to see."

"See, Mama?" I say as we check our books out.
"I like books – that's what matters. Not what they're about.

And don't worry," I add. "I know this one by heart.
I can read it to you – all the way from the start."